MW01674977

Oh Well, I Thought

by JoVonne

DORRANCE
PUBLISHING CO
EST. 1920
PITTSBURGH, PENNSYLVANIA 15238

The contents of this work, including, but not limited to, the accuracy of events, people, and places depicted; opinions expressed; permission to use previously published materials included; and any advice given or actions advocated are solely the responsibility of the author, who assumes all liability for said work and indemnifies the publisher against any claims stemming from publication of the work.

Dorrance Publishing Co
585 Alpha Drive
Suite 103
Pittsburgh, PA 15238
Visit our website at *www.dorrancebookstore.com*

ISBN: 978-1-6470-2538-0
eISBN: 978-1-6470-2662-2

Acknowledgments

First, to God my Creator, and to Jesus my Savior, and the Holy Spirit my keeper; I am so grateful for grace and mercy. To my angel, who is my mother, Doretha F. Best. To the gifts that God has gifted me, my three children, LoVon, Maurice Jr., and Marcell, love has no beginning, neither does it end when it to comes to you three. My grandchildren who makes my heart beat. My siblings Lolita, Dwayne, Anthony, Demetrius, and Alisa how grateful I am to share this book with you. To my nieces and nephews, Aunt Boo always just wanted to be the best example before you. Linda, our friendship no matter how far apart is filled with love and trust. Dezma, Wanda, Ness, Fern, Barbara, Priscilla, and Denise, ladies, love is who we are, thank you. To these wonderful people I met on the job didn't know that work came with such a bonus: LaShan, Christina, Cassandra, Carlton my brother, LaDonna, Shela, Teresa, Aletha, Dexter, and both Vickies, thanks for all the encouraging words. To my Aunt Lucy, my kisses and hugs do I send to you. To my forever mentor, Barbara Blackwell, thank you for all your support. To the memory of some special ones gone but never forgotten: my brothers, Earl, William, and baby brother Don Diego. Chandra Bailey, Willie Mae Thorpe, and Mary Davis, know that I love and miss you. My Godchildren Gerald Lassiter Jr. and Sierra Simpkins and extended family; the Thomases, Baileys, and Prices, thank you.

To the butterflies who continue to fly around me, Ms. Mamie Tinsley and Mrs. Bailey, I feel your love. Towanda and Nettie, my big sisters who God handpicked for me, thank you ladies for lifting me up to my cousin Damita, nothing but love, and to everyone who has been encouraging and supportive to me throughout the years I humbly say thank you. To the editors and publishers, my true gratitude.

Cousin Tina, you told me, "If you don't forgive, then you can never live." I have chosen to live, you continue to RIP. Lastly, Paul, Farah, and Theresa how do I say thank you, with love.

If I could encourage or uplift one person, then writing this book will never be in vain. Life goes on even through the toughest and the worst times; however, love can find you again.

Prelude

Come and go with me as we walk into two people's lives who never thought that it was possible to love again, one who enjoyed sex and wild sex was even better than the other who lived her life in fairytale land. The harsh reality was, she lost in love. That first marriage was a real fairytale until the day her world collapsed. She realized then there was no Cinderella, the Prince will not be searching until the golden slipper appears, Sleeping Beauty would not be awakened just from a mere kiss, Frozen you wish love could revive you, and the ice breaks, and my God, who rides into the sunset and lives happily ever after? I thought I had the best husband; I just wanted my wife to be the image that I always imagined her. Her appearance after the birth of the children was too much for me to bear. Never did I think about how she felt. I only knew the type of woman I wanted in my arms.

Beverly and Fredrick, two people who thirsted for love and lost love in different ways, would one day meet. Instantly they both felt attracted to one another. After the accident, they began to fantasize and, at times lusted at the thought of being with each other. Is there really chemistry the first time you meet? Beverly and Fredrick both had issues that they both wanted to erase.

Fredrick's company was now well known, and other companies were starting to reach out. Beverly was the Associated Director of HR, in the finance department, they were both just fine. With their children they both were doing alright, now with those exes' major issues you have Beverly, who never understood why her husband thought she was a liar, and Fredrick, through his selfishness and unrealistic standards, lost a beautiful woman. Their hidden secrets they wanted to keep just that, a secret. But to love and live again some secrets must be broken. Despite it all, life can have a fairytale ending if the truth be told in the beginning.

Contents

Introduction

Beverly Hollywood

Let me tell you something about myself other than being beautiful just the way I am. I am golden brown, curvy, busty, like to wear my hair natural and short, but, now and then will give you a change just to surprise and excite you. Me, I like the red hair; love the blonde hair, both bring a sex appeal, a glow, a radiance that keeps me illuminated and alive. I am not quiet, however, not loud and outrageous, just fun and more fun, that's me.

As a child, I thought I would grow up to be a star with fame and fortune, my name all in lights, film, and television. I thought that when I came back to the neighborhood, I would be in a driven limousine, bringing gifts to my family and friends. I never thought about what I was going to do to fulfill this dream. I forgot about how I needed to stay focused and should have begun to prepare myself in that direction. You see, life became a ball of fun doing what I wanted to do. I never forgot my dreams, but I didn't pursue them either.

What's up, my name is Fredrick Chase.

I am six feet tall, middle brown-skinned brother with big green eyes, a vibrant bright smile that sends the women mad, and yet I am lonely.

I thought that if you found that special woman and married her, then you would be happy forever. My world, her world, our world completed. That beautiful face, that sexy body, her contagious laughter; her love for me should have been enough and mine for her. I was wrong; after the children change, significant changes, I couldn't handle them. I wanted her to look the same; becoming a plus-size woman was not the woman I wanted in my arms.

I thought if I looked elsewhere, then maybe I could love as I loved her, just highly mistaken it has been relationship after relationship. Finally, I even tried settling for second best and even that was unfulfilling. Can I love another the way I loved her, can I ever hold another the way I caressed her, can I kiss another the way I kissed her, can my heart smile the way it smiled with her? The Bible says for those who have found themselves a wife have found a good thing.

Life-Changing Encounter

Beverly

Monday 5:45 A.M., I got time to work out before I start my day. I'm not sure how I ended up in such a rut going to a 9-to-5 job, Monday through Friday. Oh, I remember LOVE, I fell for it, let me tell you...."

Suddenly a voice hollers from the other room. "Hey, Momma! Hey, Momma!"

"What, what!!!"

Sorry for the interruption; did I mention children? School just started; they need to get dressed and I am about to prepare breakfast. Instead of having a maid or butler, mmm, I'm the domestic one.

Everybody fasten your seatbelts, and let's go.

"Twins, this is a new school year. I expect big things. You know, next school year you will be in high school, aww, my babies."

They both look and say, "Mom, please stop with the gushy stuff," and we all laughed.

Slowly we pull up to John F. Mays Middle School in District Hgts., MD.

"Bye, Mom, enjoy your day," comes first from Don Diego.

"Love you, Mommy," says Darcell Summer.

I blow them a kiss and off I go to work. I decide to go another way. I have plenty of time and you know sometimes the best thing for me is to get into the car and ride.

(Thinking aloud, Beverly starts talking about her parenting skills.)

I thought that if I focused on my children and were extra nurturing, they would see how much Mommy loves and adores them despite all that has happened in our lives. I thought that at times I would never encounter so much sadness, disappointments, rudeness, and disrespectfulness from the two bundles of joy that I carried inside of me for nine months. I thought that parenting meant gratification, I thought that our times together were so precious, and yet at times I just wanted to pack up and run. Their dad he isn't an absentee dad, but his distaste for me made it hard to communicate. Why couldn't I shake him and erase him? I tried for years. He had no problem erasing me. Love, I wholeheartedly, fell for love, marriage I treasured. I can't say that I am lonely, but at times I feel so alone.

Fredrick

(riding in the same direction)

Man, I had a wild night that Sharon is memorable wow. I wish I loved her, but after what Maria said to me I am not sure if I want to ever be with one woman solely. Last night was about fulfillment and affection, leave out the love, but the sex was still amazing. Maria told me after I had asked her out that she was not spending as much time with me because she didn't want to be bunned up (meaning together so much); however, it was alright when I was married. She went as far as to say to me that I was married, and she only wanted to see if she could control me, and yes, I took the bait. She told me that I didn't care about my marriage or family, so why would she want a dog like me permanently? "You loved that woman, and yet you still destroyed your family, all because she gained weight after having bored your children, that could have happened to me." She silenced me to the point of shame and humiliation, and my thoughts became cloudy. I found myself over and over asking myself, what was I thinking, all these years, how did I miss it? We went out, and now when I thought it would be something spectacular, she tells me, "You should have kept your wife." (Bending over and not paying attention to the road, he puts a CD in to play.) BANG. I am going to stop driving these old cars.

Damn, messing with that CD, I hit someone's car.

(Fredrick jumps out of his car.)

"I am sorry, are you okay, are you okay?"

Beverly says, "I think so, let me just get myself together, give me a few seconds."

Fredrick goes back to his car and waits, not knowing if the young lady has suffered any injury due to his negligence. He then gets back out of the car and walks over to her car and asks again, "Are you okay? I am so sorry; my name is Fredrick Chase. Here are my insurance information and my business card. Please don't hesitate to call; I was in the wrong."

She says, "You didn't see me?"

Somewhat ignoring her, he says, "We should call our jobs to inform them of the accident."

She says, "Okay, I will," so at that time, she calls her job. Beverly was the first one in the office, so therefore she leaves a message and emails the job.

Fredrick calls his long-time secretary. Shirley answers the telephone and recognizes the call is coming from his cell phone.

"Good morning, Fred."

"Shirley, not so good. I have caused an accident and must stay on the scene and wait for clearance."

Shirley asks Fredrick, are you alright?

"Yes, it was just a fender bender. Shirley, can you please cancel all my appointments for today and reschedule them for next Monday? Thank you, I will call you later."

"Bye, Fred."

"Bye, Shirley."

"Excuse me, I do see that you have minor damages. Should I call for a tow truck?" Fredrick says caringly.

"No, sir, I think that I can make it home."

At that time, Fredrick begins to hold his hand. Beverly asks him if he is alright.

"It looks as though you need to go to the doctor's office right now."

"What is your name?"

"Sorry, my name is Beverly Hollywood."

"Mrs. Hollywood...."

"No, just Miss."

"Well, Miss Hollywood, I have other cars and from the look of it, you might need a car."

"Thank you for the offer, but I can get my mother's car or a friend's. Besides, I don't know you well enough to drive your car; however, the offer was so kind."

"Miss Hollywood, I know this sounds crazy, can I get your telephone number?"

Beverly thinks for a second. *Why not? Then I know his information is accurate.* (She gives him her number) Now you go and get that hand checked out, and no matter what, let me know what the doctor did or had to say about your hand." Beverly says I am concern about you, "Can you still drive?"

"Yes," answers Fredrick, and suggests that Beverly too should be checked out.

Beverly looks at him, then responds, "Maybe later. For now I will pop these pills and go home and relax. However, you go and take care of yourself."

Fredrick nods as he leaves, holding his hand. At that point, the pain is like a toothache. Fredrick had also texted Bob, his friend, asking him to meet at his house; from that point, drive him to the; hospital.

That night Beverly only thinks about the handsome guy that had offered one of his cars and asked for her phone number.

Fredrick

That night Fredrick cannot get Beverly out of his mind. He says to himself, "She's a thick girl, just not my type of woman. But she looked amazing in that black pantsuit trimmed in pink. Why am I so focused on Miss Hollywood? After all, I should be resting my broken wrist. I did tell her that I would give her a call, letting her know my diagnosis, but not tonight. I am a player, that is the card I will use to play her, my broken wrist. Hahaha!!"

Real Talk with the Ladies

I am so tired and worn out, but I know that tonight is girls' night out and I have a lot to talk about, who has a fender bender and the guy is a complete gentleman and he is so fine, yep, tonight I got something to say. Ouch, my knee is hurting. I need to try losing a few pounds, first by watching what I eat.

"Hello, Mom," I hear as I walk into the house.

"Hello, Darcell Summer, what a vision of loveliness. Where is Don Diego? Did he finish his homework?"

She replies, "Yes, he did," then he grabs that basketball and goes outside.

I sure hope he brings us money one day, show him a ball and he will play.

"Mom, several of your girlfriends have been calling you. Is there something in church tonight?"

"No, it's girls' night out and we are going to exhale."

Darcell starts to laugh. "Who will you be talking about, Mom?"

"Why?"

As I run upstairs to shower and revive myself, I decide to slip on jeans and my phenomenal women t-shirt. Darcell remains downstairs. I can hear her say, "She just wants to tell everybody about that man from the accident."

I say to myself, "Yes, real talk, how many women get into a fender bender and the man wants their number, plus offers one of his cars? Say what you want, not many people, honey, nope, not many."

"Is that the door I hear?"

"Yes, Mom, it is me, your fine son."

I laugh and say, "Hello, my fine son. I will be down in a few, just putting on a little makeup. You'll pop in a microwave dinner, or there are some leftovers, but I got to go. Love you guys."

"Drive safely, Mom, and enjoy girls' night out."

"Thank you," I say, running toward my car.

On my way to Patricia's house, I turn down 5th Street and go up Lollipop Drive. As I am pulling into the driveway, I notice that several cars are already in the driveway. I ring the doorbell and Patricia answers.

"Hello, Beverly, come in and take your seat."

Patricia is most pleasant and she looks very nice with this long African lounger and a scarf to match, but what I find odd about Patricia is that most women or girls whose name is Patricia you call Pat, not her. She said that she was named Patricia and that is the name she prefers to be called.

Patricia says, "Are you ready to cry, laugh and, yes, exhale? Ladies, we will first open in prayer. 'Lord, we come before you in friendship and in love to exhale, not to be messy or judgmental to one another, and know that what we reveal here in this room stays in this room, Amen.'"

Patricia says, "We are still waiting for two more ladies, will give them about three to five minutes, then we will get started. In the meantime, please feel to free to enjoy the refreshments."

Ness is a petite dark-skinned woman with a figure-8 body, and Patti is a large woman with a voice like an angel and dresses as though she is size 2, not 22, makeup as though she is an artist, beautiful, and then there is Monica Bell, who has a smile that lights up the room.

Time has gone by and the other two ladies have not arrived, so Patricia opens the floor. "Who has something to say, but remember, real talk."

At that time, Monica Bell says she would begin talking about that smile and how it has always been so inviting but never the right guy. She tells about a recent relationship/fling, how she felt worthless, I mean down-to-the-ground worthless.

Monica Bell starts to talk about her outer appearance. "I am a slender woman with long black hair and light-colored eyes, pretty, and sadly very unsure of myself. I have never been married, but all my relationships have lasted at least two years nothing good or promising has come from any relationship only material items. A friendship diamond ring, a car, paying my rent, and yet no one has ever asked my hand in marriage. This last guy just told me to my face, 'Yes, you are good to look at, good to have on a man's arm, good to lay with, but not a wife.' Then he had the nerve to say, 'I want a woman of value.' What the hell did he think I was for two years? I am a 32-year-old young woman, and I have loved me all these years, and this man comes along and tears down my self-worth! I have been questioning and wondering, did all the men in my past think and feel the same about me?"

As she cries, we all get up to embrace her; Ness says "No, you continue to stand like a proud peacock."

Patricia is very faired-skinned with what you would call good hair and extremely busty and the only one with a husband who just adores her. Patricia says, "Real talk. I have been married for eight years, and my husband decided to tell me that he wants a child. I had a hysterectomy at the age of 16 after being hit by a car. I told him that upfront, so for him to ask me about a child is heartbreaking. I told him all about me ten years ago. I love my life as it is, but he has suggested that we adopt a child or two."

Then I start to cry because her story is so like mine, and yet I can never bring myself to talk about that half of my life. Again, we stop to hug her as well.

Patricia says with tears in her eyes, "Real talk, is there anyone else?"

"Me, I have something to say."

Everyone looks at me because tonight, I too have something to share.

So, I begin to tell about the little accident and how this man offered me his car and then wanted to get my number. I told them, "For years I have been so afraid to go out with a guy, but to know that a man still sees me as attractive where at times I had given up on meeting or dating." I am so excited. "No, he has not called but I feel that he would."

The ladies start screaming and shouting out, "What! What does he look like, where does he work, and tell us more and more?"

I say again, "He hasn't called, so I can't answer your questions, but this time I was not afraid to give my number."

"Oh, how does he look, is he a gorgeous Hulk of a specimen?" says Ness. "Girl, he offered you his car so that you would not spend any of your money or use your insurance, nice and classy type of guy. I hope something comes out of this; you deserve happiness."

"Thank you, Ness, what sweet words."

Next, it is Ness who takes the floor. She talks about losing her girlfriend. "I miss her, her voice, that laughter, our serious conversations, our funny conversations, we were friends over thirty years."

"She is always with you," says Patti.

Ness looks and says, "Thank you," as tears stream down her cheeks. She begins to say, "I thought as we grew old together, we would be able to reminisce about our teens, our early adulthood, and when we became older our bodies and faces. I never thought about death, how it robs you of so many more memories. *Oh well*, I thought."

Patti then takes the floor. "I just thought that no man worthwhile would want to go out with me, so I settled for the hustlers, the ballers, the shot callers, and found nothing but sadness and sometimes abusiveness, but God showed me better. I was more than just a quick piece of ass, sorry, don't want to use the word butt. I want to say what was said to me all too often, 'Bring that oversized ass over here.' I would smile and give it up; I just thought that I was not worthy having a man who knows how to respect and love me. I took the gifts; I took the money. I wanted to believe that these things meant he loved me. *Oh well*, I thought."

Then we all say, "Thank God you have changed, and Jesus is your Man now."

Patti says, "Right on!"

We say a prayer to close out girls' night, and Patricia gives instructions for the next girls' night. She tells us to come with something that we have been embarrassed about but need to get it out, "And if you are not willing to share, then please don't join us, everyone has to participate. At the end of the talk, no words will we exchange; everyone will hug and leave. Then the next girls' night, we will talk only about victories that you have overcome and how God saw you through them, gave you the strength to endure." Patricia then says, "Finish the refreshments, and see you all next time for 'real talk.'"

Momma, I Need You

The day after girls' night, I am still so excited just to share what happened to me. Realty wise I have not heard from Fred Chase, but he is a man of his word; my car has been repaired and paid. Well, I will not dwell on this anymore. If Mr. Chase calls, then I will talk to him; if not, then I am still alright. God, will I love and trust again? I believe God, and therefore it is His will, and He will guide me to the perfect man who is worthy of my love. Why did he ask for my number? It has been a long time since I dated or talked to a guy. He looked at these vivacious curves, these full bosoms, and I hope he only saw me. I didn't smile because of the situation, but if I ever get to meet him again in person, he will get these $5000 teeth and my million-dollar smile, oh yes. (Like a silly schoolgirl, she chuckled. As quick as she thought about the encounter, she also thinks about her ex-husband and what if one day she is asked about him.)

Beverly, you are jumping the gun (Beverly tries to calm down), but already I am anxious if he or any man asks about my past. How do I begin to tell about a man who I thought loved me and yet destroyed me? The man I married was a successful architect, designing the most decorative, modernized, and futuristic buildings around the world. He would call me from anywhere, "I will be flying you out this weekend to join me," how I loved it and how I loved him. I took off a week, and he flew me to London. As we walked and talked that night, I knew I would be telling him the best news he had ever received, so I thought. The night was full of passion as he gently kissed me from head to toe and made love to me for hours until we both fell asleep in each other's arms. In the morning, the passionate lovemaking continued and, again, we fell asleep. When we finally got ourselves together, we hopped out of bed, and we both took showers, then decided to order room service for our brunch. Marvin said, "What's on your mind?" I ran over, hopped in his lap, and said, "We are going to be parents."

"WHO IN THE HELL ARE GOING TO BE PARENTS!!!! I told you when I met you no, children and if that is what you wanted, then find someone else."

With tears, I got up from his lap. "Marvin, all my young teenage years and young adult, life I was told no children because of painful periods and pelvic inflammatory disease. I told you this Baby this is a miracle from God."

"No," he said, "this is bullshit, so get rid of it now."

I looked at him, he looked at me and said, "The fun is over, call the airline and see if you can go back home today, no matter what it costs to change your flight, and when I get back in two weeks, the procedure had better have been taken care of bye, Beverly."

I did as he said, to numb even cry, too shocked to speak a word. Let me get the hell away from this monster.

POEM

I thought

I thought marriage was forever, I thought that true love never dies, I thought that tears would be tears of joy and not so much sorrow.

I thought the minister said let no man put asunder, I thought that children were a gift from God and sealed our family.

Oh well, I thought

When I arrived home so sad, so in disbelief, so traumatized—yep, traumatized was the word.

When Tuesday came, I went onto the internet to find a place. No way could I go to my regular doctor's office. Monday, I cried and cried, how could he demean and shame me about the lives we created out of love? That he ordered me to end the pregnancy.

I found Dr. June Staples; she worked at Stone Wall's Women's Clinic. The receptionist's voice was calming. She asked if I had insurance. I said, "I do but will be paying with cash for this visit." She then told me the price of the visit, and she showed me the cost of the procedures.

"Please have a seat; someone will be calling you from the door on the left." Thank you, I said.

As the door opened, the medical assistant called out, "Mrs. Hollywood?"

I answered, "Yes?"

"Please come with me. Mrs. Hollywood, please put your things on the chair. I need to take your blood pressure and your weight."

The medical assistant also told me that she would need to draw blood and have the sample tested in the lab. She then said, no need to worry, just a precaution to verify your pregnancy. Ms. Hollywood, it will take up to an hour for the results. At that time, Dr. Staples will come in to examine you.

After about an hour, the doctor came in the room. We greeted one another; then, she told me that she needed to examine me to determine how far along I was into the pregnancy. I informed the doctor that my intentions were not to continue with the pregnancy. It was at that time the doctor told me that I would be aborting two fetuses because I was having twins.

I looked at her and started crying so hard that she asked me to have a seat and get myself together. I didn't tell the doctor everything, but I did let her know that my husband wanted to abort. Yelling, "How can I, how can I? I just cannot destroy my babies."

I was crying, screaming, and filled with emotions that I then ran out of that clinic. The medical assistant was calling my name.

"Mrs. Hollywood, please calm down."

When I finally got home, my eyes were shut closed from crying, and fear had crept inside of me. One, I knew the marriage was over. Secondly, this was a miracle, I would not give the babies up, God blessed me, and God will take care of me.

Later on that evening, I called my mother. When my mother said hello, I just cried and cried.

"He called me a liar, and he does not want his children."

My mother said, "Calm down, please calm down, Bev. I thought you were in London."

"Nope, Marvin told me to get on whatever flight I could but get the hell away from him."

Momma said, "I am on my way over to your house."

When she arrived, that lady brought hell in there with her.

"Where is he! Where is he! If he thinks that he can address my child in that matter? He is a small man; I never cared for him; he thinks that he is all of that because you love him. I have put up with his shit!!!"

As hurt, as I was my mother, carried on so badly, I was laughing until I cried all over again. She didn't use curse words.

"Lady, he is not here for one, and you need to calm down."

She said, "I am ready to whip his ass. This time he has gone way too far."

As I began to tell my mother what all had taken place, my mother then cried and said, "I am going to be a grandmother. If he doesn't want you all I am willing to sell my house and we'll buy a bigger house for all of us." Then Momma shouted, "Glory to God, this is your handywork, Lord, and you have blessed her, grateful am I."

My mother stayed with me the next two nights, and we talked about everything.

"It is your choice ultimately, and you decide for you." Momma said, "Beverly, I am sorry to say but your marriage or these children, that is the choice I am more than sure Marvin will be putting before you."

The following Monday, Marvin came home from London. As I turned the key and slightly opened the door, I heard the TV. Once inside, he looked up at me, and I looked at him. No words were exchanged no kisses, no "Baby, I missed you," nothing. He said nothing to me and I had nothing to say to him.

"Did you call the doctor's office and did you make the final arrangement?" He chopped at me.

I looked at him and said, "Hell no, I am carrying twins, and if you think that I am going to get rid of my babies, then you are mistaken. I will pack me some clothes for the rest of the week and will be at my mother's. Marvin, as much as I do love you, sorry, I can't give them up, not even for you."

I left and went to my mother's and stayed that whole week. After work each evening, I returned to her place. I thought about my life and my future, and right then I had no answers.

After that week, I went back home, unaware of what I would be facing. Marvin looked at me, and again I looked at him. He only said this: "You have decided to keep these children. You have made it clear you have also decided to live without me."

"No, Marvin, I said you have decided to live without us."

"Beverly, whatever the case, I will be with you throughout the pregnancy. I will be there to see my children born, and I will take care of them. But you and I will never be the same, and eventually, I am leaving you for lying. You said that you could not have children and lady, you are now having twins."

I hollered at him and said, "I am not a liar; I know what I've been told for years."

From that point on, nothing was said other than "hello" and maybe, "how are you feeling?" He did ask about the doctor's appointments, and strangely, he attended each one.

One evening I overheard him on the phone, telling his mother how he felt about becoming a dad, how his father was absent and never showed him nor his siblings any love. "I will not be that kind of dad, Mom, that I promise you. Beverly betrayed me, and it is too much to handle. At this point the marriage is over!" I heard him say, "I mean what I said, I wanted a wife I can trust, and I no longer have that kind of wife."

He noticed that I was standing in the doorway and could hear his conversation with his mother. He did nothing to ease my pain, so slowly, I walked away hurt but finally getting how this man whom I loved and admired felt. He was standing on his conviction that I was a liar.

As the months rolled by and I became so huge, we prepared for the baby shower. We knew that they were boy and girl, so the colors reflected. Marvin wore blue for the boy, and I wore pink for the girl. Both our families showed in great numbers. My mother had nothing to say to Marvin; she didn't even say hello. She greeted his family as though nothing was going on; his family all hugged me. We played games; we opened many gifts; we even took pictures together; for those hours I wished I could have kept in a bottle.

One night I tossed and turned when pain like no other hit me. I called his name, "Marvin, please come, I am in pain."

Marvin came out of the next room; by that time, we were sleeping in separate rooms. He called the doctor and timed the contractions. He was very good. Next, we were on our way to be parents, good or bad, happy or sad.

The delivery was not long but it was hard. After three hours I knew that my life would change as I knew it. There they were, so beautiful and healthy and mine. Each baby weighed in at 6 pounds. Don Diego had all the hair, Darcell Summer had none. I noticed that Marvin was following the nurses to ensure that the babies were safe.

After arriving home with the twins, the atmosphere was totally different. Marvin really helped with the babies, putting in maternity leave for six weeks with his job. We did agree that I took off at least six months. However, his attitude toward me remained cold and, at times, frosty, but we managed.

As the babies grew in months, then years, the finalization hit home. The white picket fence gone, the big beautiful well-designed house lost the feeling of home gone, the love as husband and wife gone.

One day it happened.

"Beverly," Marvin said in a very stern-like voice. "The marriage is over, I will be divorcing you."

I gave him no answer, no body language, just a little stare, then walked away.

Later, after putting the twins down for a nap, I thought about Marvin and my beginning, how it was full of love, fun, and joy, then sadly I thought of the here and now, gloom and doom. No fairytale ending for me. *Oh well,* I thought.

Six months later, Marvin did leave. At the time the twins were three years old. He came to me and said, "Beverly, I have leased an apartment near my mother. As for the house, it is best that we sell and split the money. Unless you want to buy me out or remove my name and refinance in your name solely."

Looking at him, I wanted to scream; I wanted to fight him, I wanted to cuss him out. Instead, in front of him I cried.

He showed no compassion. "Beverly, I will take care of my children. I will also have my attorney draw up some legal papers on what I am willing to contribute; however, if you have any objections, then I would suggest you seek an attorney. Just another suggestion," he stated, "my sister is a realtor. She can help you find a place, along with helping us sell this place. Beverly," he said again as though he was calling all the shots, "once the proposal is drawn the ball will be rolling, meaning we will proceed with the divorce. There will no longer be a need to pretend that we are together."

Well, I never hired an attorney. Marvin lived up to every piece of his commitment, even increasing the monthly child support I guessed when he got a raise.

Marvin never forgave me, and all transactions went into the joint account that we once shared. I thought to myself, *I haven't seen him in years. His family picks up the children and his family returns the children back home. I thank God nothing serious ever happened,* still thinking how I was married to a peculiar man who happened to be an amazing father.

As I am thinking and talking aloud, I go into my closet and pull out an envelope. There I see the proposal letter that was drawn. After fifteen years, why am I still embarrassed? Father, God, I ask for strength to one day tell someone, I mean anyone, about what happened with my marriage.

(She held up the proposal, read it, shook her head, and buried it deep in the closet again.)

The Proposal of Child Support

Attorney: Edward Nelson
Edward Nelson and Edward Nelson Jr.
Client: Marvin S. Hollywood

Child Support for Don Diego and Darcell Summer Hollywood

- $2,000.00 monthly
- Healthcare and Dental will be covered by Mr. Hollywood.
- Daycare cost will be split between Mr. Hollywood and ex-wife Beverly Hollywood.
- Holidays – Rotation
- Visitation – Every weekend only because he travels so much during the week
- Summertime
- Two weeks but Miss Hollywood can give the dates in advance and she can break up the 2 weeks as well.

He Saw the Light

After months, Fredrick is surprised that he still has this woman on his mind. To himself, he thinks, *I want to call her so bad, I can't believe it, she is not normally my type of woman. I have not been able to get her out of my mind. This is mind-blowing to me.* It has been months since the accident (he begins to look through his wallet for her number) as he stares at her phone number. *Should I or shouldn't I give her a call today? I need to let her know that my wrist was broken; at least I can call and tell her that much.*

He starts to dial the number. Ring, ring, then someone says, "Hello?"

"Uh, yes, hello, this is Fredrick Chase. I am trying to reach Ms. Beverly Hollywood."

"This is she."

"Again, this is Fredrick Chase, not sure if you remember me, but I am the crazy guy who ran into your car," he says.

"Yes, and thank you for being a man of your word. Everything was taken care of and paid for by you," Beverly responds. "Let me ask you something, how is your arm?"

"Beverly, my wrist was broken, so I am calling to give you an update. Let me be honest, I have been thinking about you ever since the accident. You never screamed or got out hollering, calling me names, you displayed a very calm and reserved demeanor, and I truly was at fault. You know, Ms. Hollywood, you have a glow about you, a light that just shines so bright."

"Thank you, and to be open with you I too have been thinking about you, Mr. Chase."

Fredrick then asks Beverly if they can get together and just talk.

Beverly just doesn't want to appear desperate, so she says, "Can I think about that, Fredrick?"

Fredrick, not sure how to answer, says, "Okay."

Quickly Beverly answers. "Well, I thought it over and that would be nice."

Fredrick says, "Let me check my calendar and see what day I am clear, Beverly, I own my own company, and at times I have no time to go out or have a good conversation with anyone."

"Sounds fair," Beverly replies. "I'll wait to hear back from you sooner than later."

"Goodbye, Beverly."

"Goodbye, Fredrick."

Two days later Fredrick calls. "Beverly, this Saturday is clear for me. What does your schedule look like?"

Beverly says, "In the morning a little busy, but I will be clear around 11:30 A.M."

Fredrick says, "Great, let's meet around 1:00 P.M."

We both confirm, Saturday is a go. That Saturday morning both of us are anxious and excited at the same time, palms sweating, nervous energy, and yet ready and hoping for a new beginning.

It is the first day of fall. The summer is still lingering in the air, so it is a mixture, summer by day and fall by night. The day is going to be a spectacular day. Mr. Chase will be seeing me for the first time since the accident. I wish I could lose thirty pounds right now, my hair looks a mess. I tell myself to calm down and stop the negativity. This is what you wanted, so girl, put on a wig, a body shaper, and that smile.

The phone rings.

"Good morning, this is Fredrick. Are you ready for an amazing day?"

I answer, "Yes, I am Fredrick," I then say with caution, "can today be amazing without any serious questions?"

Fredrick says, "Fine with me, let our day be a day of fun, so Beverly, how much fun can you handle in one day?"

I answer, "All that you can bring my way."

Fredrick says, "All set, lady. I will see you at 1:00 P.M. Goodbye until then."

"Okay," I say, "I will see you then."

I go to my closet. This will be a jean and sexy top kind of a day. I will bring a jacket just in case the date goes into tonight.

We both agree that we will meet in a place near me but not my home. I do give Don Diego and Darcell Summer both his name and numbers. I also tell them that I will be texting them the type of car and his tag number.

I am the first to arrive, although Fredrick is not late. He drives up in a white convertible, the top is not down, although it is that kind of day.

Fredrick gets out of the car, what an eye-opener, fine, I mean fine. I study him a while, just like a shark, my jaws want to eat him.

As he looks around, "Excuse me, are you looking for me?" I ask in a playful manner. "Hello, Mr. Chase?"

Smiling he says, "Yes, I am, lady."

We give each other a quick embrace, and both stand there smiling at one another.

Finally, Fredrick says, "Let's go have lunch first." He had made reservations for two at the most exquisite restaurant in town. "Beverly, you order whatever meal your taste buds desire, and I will order my favorite meal."

"Do you frequent this place much?" I ask.

"At one time I did, the food is delicious," Fredrick replies. "Beverly, after this I have tickets to an amateur comedy show," Fred says, "let's get our laugh on! Miss Hollywood, you are beautiful just as I remembered."

"Please don't make me blush," I giggle, returning the compliment. "You too are just as I remembered, handsome, no, let me say it correctly, man, you are fine."

Fredrick says bashfully, "So now that is out of the way, let's enjoy our lunch."

After eating and basking on good conversation that could have lasted all day, Fred suggests that both cars should be parked in a garage and not on the street because of the time we would be away. Fredrick also says, "All expenses I will be covering on this date."

I think to myself, *Look at this dude, not only did he pay for the repairs on my car, he is now paying for the whole day, including parking.*

Hours had elapsed as we walk back to the garage, still laughing and repeating some of the punchlines that were said in the comedy show. I suddenly stop, turn to Fredrick, and begin to thank him. "Fredrick, I told you during lunch, it has been a while since I have been in the company of a man. Today, I prayed and asked God, 'Please allow me to enjoy this date,' and I have had the best time. Fred, although the evening must come to an end, I hope that my company with you has been just as fabulous."

I can tell that I have stunned him a little because he stutters before answering, "Uh, uh, truly I have enjoyed this day and this time with you," then he thinks to himself, *Even if I didn't enjoy myself with this breath of loveliness, no ill words could I utter out of my mouth.* At that time, Fredrick says, "Beverly, I would like to do this again and again. Fredrick, now somewhat serious, tells Beverly, "before we go any further, I think we need to talk about who we are, our past lives, and what we want in the future. Today was awesome, I feel something when I am around you and I think you do too, so let's have that talk not over the telephone, not texting but face to face."

With hesitation I respond, "Okay, that sounds fair," but inside I am trembling.

Fred says, "I will check my calendar or see what day I am not working so late." Fred too is trembling inside. Fredrick takes my hand and says, "We both need to exhale, as you women prefer to say to one another, no secrets, no lies, at that time if we feel about each other the way we do right now, then we can go forth, no judging or badgering each other with additional questions."

I say, "Who determines how much we need to say?"

"Baby, you make that choice," says Fredrick. "Beverly, this is just an opening of doors that have been shut and whether these doors be reopened or remain closed." He then kisses me on the cheek and says, "Please text or call me to let me know that you made it home safely."

"I will, Fredrick, but you do the same. Goodnight."

That night when I arrive home, I take a shower and try to focus on reading a book while waiting to hear from Fredrick. The phone rings, and it is Fredrick letting me know that he has arrived home safety.

I tell him, "So glad you made it home, so what are you going to do now?"

"Well, pretty lady, I have several meetings on Monday. So for the rest of the night, until I fall asleep, I will be reading and in between thinking about you. I have new companies that I am hoping to bring aboard. Researching and reading are the tools for preparing; I will be ready."

"Fredrick, I see you have an agenda, so I will let you go, goodnight again."

"Goodnight to you as well, my special lady," and just like that he hangs up the phone.

"Special lady," I jump up and down, "he called me his special lady." That night I lay down and have the biggest smile planted on my face.

The next morning, I am still in awe as I prepare myself for church service. I begin to thank God for allowing such an evening and say, "Lord, if that was my last day of happiness, what a day!"

Fredrick tells his best friend

When church is over, Richard, known as Rick, sees Fredrick. "Hi, Fred, what is up for the rest of the afternoon?"

"I have a few new companies that I will be meeting with, hoping to bring them on board, so I am quite busy for the rest of the day. Rick, I do need to talk to you, man, you know that young lady who I ran into with my car?"

"Yep," he replies.

"Yesterday we had our first date."

"Fred, how did it go?"

"Rick, man, extremely well, good conversation, lots of laughing, I just didn't want the evening to end," Fred says to Rick.

Then teasing, Rick replies to Fred, "You are just like me, we like them thick and fine."

Giggling, Fred says, "Whatever, man, she is beautiful, and I want her to be mine, all mine. You know, Rick, God has a way of showing us how ignorant we can be, and how our mistakes can leave us empty and lonely. Anyway, man, how is your wife?"

Rick responds, "Just lovely, we will be celebrating our third wedding anniversary in the island."

"Which one?" Fred asks.

"Fred, I don't know, the cruise ship lands on several islands according to the package we chose, okay, correction, Nicole selected. Fred, keep this on a hush until later, Nicole is expecting, please keep it hush-hush, we are supposed to remain silent until she reaches four months."

"Congratulations!" and Fred is about to hug Rick when Rick says, "Man, I know I told you this was hush-hush, wait until we hang out, man, you have been the same way since we met as teenagers, always overreacting. Anyway, man," says Rick, "have I ever thanked you for such a wild bachelor party and all the works?"

"No," Fred says while looking at Rick, "but I guess three years later is never too late, you are welcome."

The two men laugh and shake each other's hands.

"See you later, Fred. The next nice day, let's ride our bikes?"

"That is a bet," says Fred as he walks away.

Beverly

After a glorious church service, I ask my mother if she cooked Sunday dinner, and if so, can I and the twins invite ourselves over for dinner?

"Well, of course, I tried calling you yesterday, but Darcell told me you were on a date."

"Yes, I can't wait to tell you, Momma. I am so excited that is the real reason I want to come over for dinner."

"By the way, what did you cook?"

"Beverly, if you must know," Karen says, "I have already prepared dinner, fresh collard greens, baked chicken and fried chicken, three Cornish hens, and macaroni and cheese, and for dessert lemon Bundt cake with lemon icing."

"Wow, Momma," I reply, "We will be over around 6:00 P.M. Momma, is that too late for you?"

"Girl, no, it gives me a chance to go home and take a nap," Karen says.

"Momma, see you later, let me start calling these children. I don't see them anywhere right now." I pull out my cell phone to call one of the twins, hoping they are together or close by one another.

On our way home from church, I tell the twins that they are going to Grandma's house for Sunday dinner.

Don Diego says, "Mom, do I have to go? Can you just bring me a plate or two?"

"Don Diego, you don't want to see Grandma?"

"Mom, that is not it, I just want to stay home."

Right when I am about to answer Don Diego, Darcell says, "I want to stay home as well."

I say, "Okay, but I am not bringing anyone a plate back, fend for yourselves."

Darcell says, "Oh, no, let me go in this house, get some rest, and gather my homework, I am going with Momma."

Don Diego looks at Darcell with puppy-like eyes. "Can you please bring me a plate?"

"I shouldn't, but I will do that just for you, brother."

"Don Diego, are you sure you don't want to go? We are leaving at 5:30 P.M."

Half asleep, he says, "No, but tell Grandma I said love her. These tryouts are kicking my butt, praying I make the team."

"Son, you will, come on, Darcell, let's go."

"Hi, Momma," I call as I open the door not to scare or startle my mom.

"Hi, Beverly, hello, Darcell."

We both speak at the same time. "Hello, Momma, hello, Grandma."

Darcell says, "I will be in the front room reading and going over my homework, call me when the food is ready."

"I will," says Karen to Darcell, "Beverly, let's talk while I am warming up the food."

"Momma, I really like him, I like him, but I am so afraid of the questions he might begin to ask me."

"Hey, Beverly, maybe it's time to really put the past behind. You have struggled and have struggled, you have been in and out of therapist after therapist offices, and you still are so broken over a failed marriage. No, not over a failed marriage, but being called a liar when it was a miracle from God. A blessing that I thought I would never be able to experience."

"Momma, tell me how and why even after all these years that Marvin has not forgiven me and still considers me manipulative and a liar."

"Beverly, I am sorry that Marvin has never come to his senses. But now you might have a chance to be happy again, your twins are growing up, and before you know it, they will be in college. Live, Beverly, you deserve to live."

"I so agree with you. I will live and not die. I am so excited about Fredrick. We had our first date on Saturday, and what fun I had, laughing like a teenage girl. It felt great and Momma, I did feel alive."

"Bev, after your father died I never lived, so don't let history repeat itself. You go out and enjoy your life. Girl, I have prayed for your healing of the mind and your broken heart. God has done it again." Momma starts praising God right there, giving him all the glory. She tells me, "I see a happy you; there is now a glow about you."

As we both laugh, I know that she is relieved. It has been a long, sad, sad road.

I then called Darcell to join us for dinner.

"Let's say grace and eat dinner. Grandma, I will bless the food," says Darcell.

After dinner, my mom and I clean the kitchen in a hurry just so we can talk some more.

"Bev, do you have a picture of him?"

"Yes, Momma, I have his picture with me."

"Bev, is this the young gentleman from the accident?"

"Yes."

"He finally called you?"

"Yes!"

At that time, I dive into my purse and show my mother his picture.

"Momma, why are you screaming?"

"Bring me some water!"

"Why do you need water?"

"Because he is hot! Beverly, is his father alive, and if so, can you introduce me? He is hot, is his father hot as well?" Then she looks at me. "Okay, and what else does he have to offer other than good looks?"

"He's successful; owns his own business, such an intelligent man. He told me that it took a while, but he is on point now. Fredrick, is divorced with two teenage children."

"When will I be meeting him?"

"Momma, give it some time; I said we just started going out and talking. I am moving into this slowly. Come on, daughter of mine, it is time to go."

"Grandma, can I take a plate of food home with me, and can I fix my brother a plate?" asks Darcell.

"Yes, you can, and Darcell, you can fix Don Diego a plate or two as well. He is a growing boy."

"No," I say, "Momma, he should have come."

"Why, I saw him in church, he gave me the biggest kiss and said that he was trying out for the basketball team and how hard it was. Beverly, don't you think he may be tired? Darcell, fix him a plate or two and please take that cake."

"Thank you, Grandma!" Darcell shouts.

Kisses and hugs are in order before leaving Momma's house.

Friendships Tested

After talking to Momma and getting her insight on how I feel about finally dating or seeing someone, I like what she said, I deserve to live. I think I will call Patricia and ask her when the next girls' night out "real talk" is.

The phone rings quite a few times, then finally I get an answer.

"Hello?" the voice says.

I say, "Hello, Patricia, is this you?" and she said yes. "This is Beverly; I was wondering when the next time you will be hosting "real talk?" I have so much to say, girl, my life has changed."

Patricia says, "Girl, I am happy for you, but I will not be holding any more of those evenings."

"What, why, I mean sorry, Patricia," I say, "I am taking back by your answer!"

Patricia says, "Yes, I know; somehow, it got back to my husband what I had said regarding having children, you know what I said, you were there."

I say, "Say this is not true, so who told? We all know that there is a code; it stays here."

Patricia says, "No, I can't tell you who, but the friendship can be no more. When I tried calling her, she had blocked my number and outright refused to talk to me. But why would she go to my husband," angrily says Patricia? "My husband came to me and told me how disappointed he was that I would talk about something so personal. Beverly, he later apologized for not considering my feelings, but the truth of the matter was all his friends was becoming dads, and for one second, he too wanted to become a father. Beverly, I too apologized to him; I thought what we said during "real talk" was confidential and a way of exhaling, never to be repeated outside of that room. Beverly, girl, I trust you, please don't repeat what we have talked about this evening. I can't handle no more drama."

"Patricia," I say, "No, I would never do such a thing; you can confide in me."

Patricia goes on to tell me that she is going to adopt two children because her husband is a wonderful man and a part of her longs for that motherly touch as well. Patricia says, "I thought that friendships meant a lot, I thought the Bible said that a friend is closer than a brother; now I understand that even friendships come with conditions."

I care not to ask her again who it was because I realize sometimes you must let the trash take itself out because what is in you will show come out of you. If that person tells Patricia's husband on her, what other damage might that person tell on another, and who are they willing to expose? I still hope that getting together will not stop, but for now, just let the dust settle.

"Wow," I say while getting into my car, "too much. Let me call Vickie and see if she is willing to go shopping with me this Saturday."

Saturday morning comes, and I pick up Vickie. She looks so adorable dressed in all white.

"Girl, I thought we were going shopping, not to an all-white party?"

Vickie smiles, then when she gets into the car, it is like a storm comes in with her. "That Michelle said that I didn't call her and that I ignored all her calls. She never asked me any questions for clarity; she became the judge and the jury. I then find out she has been calling me names, saying that I was jealous, that I was mean, all because she assumes that I never tried to reach her. I asked Vickie to slow down, what has occurred that would make her react like this? Well, the other day, my dad became ill, and I contacted Sue Ann; I tried to reach Michelle but got no answer. Michelle said that she made several attempts to contact me, and I rejected her calls."

"Vickie, you didn't tell me either," I say, "but is your dad alright?"

"He recovered just fine, thank you. Beverly, are you upset with me?"

"No, plus Sue Ann told me. Why are you still crying? I am trying to have a wonderful day."

As tears come streaming down her cheeks, I see hurt and brokenness. She doesn't understand what has happened; she says that she feels as though she has opened a bag of chocolate-covered nuts that someone forgot the chocolate. Sometimes God must close the doors, even on friendships.

Vickie looks at me and says, "I know I just didn't see that coming?"

I answer, "Our Heavenly Father knows best," and gently I put my arms around Vickie and say, "What a Friend we have in Jesus."

The Truth All Laid Out

One Saturday morning, the twins and I are sitting around looking at cartoons; they still find cartoons to be enjoyable. Afterward, I start to talk to them about their higher education.

"Now that you are in high school, have you thought about colleges or universities?"

They both say, in unison, "Yes."

Darcell says that she is not sure if she wants to go away or stay at home, Diego says the same. I express to them that I would prefer them to stay on campus, at least the first year.

At that time the phone rings.

Darcell answers. "Hello, Daddy."

Darcell has a strange look on her face because their dad never calls on the house phone. Marvin avoided me and never wanted to hear my voice or have any kind of encounter with me.

"Momma, he wants to speak with you."

Perplexed, I get the receiver. "Hello?"

Marvin can hear the hesitation in my voice; quickly, he informs me that everything is fine. "Are you alone?" he asks.

"No, the twins are here with me," I reply.

"Beverly, I really must talk, and I need the time now."

"Just like years ago, you are the boss," I say sarcastically. I ask the twins to excuse themselves, and say we will resume our conversation later.

Don Diego says, "Momma, is everything okay? Let me talk to my dad."

Pushing his hand away, I tell Diego, "Before I hang up I will give you the phone."

"Beverly," Marvin says, "it has been a long time since we talked."

"Right, so what is so pressing today?" I again say sarcastically.

"You have taken very good care of my twins, and for that I am grateful. Beverly, my actions in the past were ugly and hurtful. My broken heart, never allowed me to see or hear what you had to say. When we met, I told you no children, that I wanted a wife that I could just shower with love, gifts, and a life of pure luxury. I meant that to the core of which I stand. Yes, you told me about your medical history, I was fine, but you never said that it was a chance that you still could become pregnant. Beverly, the first three years of our marriage, was a marriage made in heaven. When you said you were pregnant...."

At that time, I want to interrupt him, but I remain calm and allow him this time.

"Beverly, anger engulfed me like fire engulfs gasoline. I wanted to accept what you said regarding your medical history, but at that time, I just could not. Beverly, it has taken me years to come to grips with first, myself. Secondly, the devastation that I caused you and our marriage.

"I took care of my twins, I loved my twins, but you, I just couldn't believe what you said, and I blocked you out and became death to your voice. Today and right now, I want to say that I am sorry. I want to say that I never stopped loving you. I want to say please forgive me; I call to apologize. You have always been a wonderful woman, an amazing mother, and your heart has always been full of good. Beverly, I don't know if you can forgive me, I no longer know you in a personal manner, but the person who I did know, she would forgive me."

I can hear his voice cracking and decide this is the time for me to speak.

"Marvin! I listened to you, now hear me. For the past 15 years I've gone to bed alone, I've cried alone, there were nights I wanted to die alone. I never made a mistake about who I married. I stood before God and said until death do us part; I searched my heart and my mind and knew that it was truly you. Then the impossible happened and it was not welcomed nor was it received well by you. I felt like a person with leprosy thrown on an island and left alone; you made me feel like I was a teenager, when the young boy got all the ass he wanted and the young girl became pregnant, he ran. I was married, in love, and at times in lust. But happier as any clown who enjoys the pleasure of putting a smile on a child's face and love in their hearts. If love had a face, it was yours." As tears roll down my cheeks I can only say, "God gets the glory. My cousin Tina said years ago, 'If you don't forgive, then you cannot live.'" My voice begins to tremble. "You see, Marvin, thank you for loving them, I mean really loving them, even when you stopped loving me. However, I never lied about my health. Marvin, I told you medically, what the doctor's told to me, God allowed the miracle. I look at them today just like 15 years ago, it is still a miracle. I never lied that is what hurts the most. I am done here, let me get Don Diego, he wants to speak with you."

As Don Diego gets the receiver I walk away, finally free.

Some nerve of him, he said that if had to choose the miracle or the wife he would have chosen the wife.

I thought that sorry would have never come, I thought that hatred and malice would forever fill his heart, I thought that forgiving him was impossible. *Oh well,* I thought.

As Don Diego is saying goodbye to his dad. I notice that his eyes are fixed on me.

"Momma, is you alright?"

"Yes, I am, I am finally alright."

Don Diego asks his dad if he can call him later. "Dad, right now I want to attend to my mother."

I tell him, "No, I am fine."

"Okay, Momma, what was that all about?"

"Diego" I say, "it was about a marriage ending, and I think that your dad should be the one you speak with, it was his decision, not mine. Diego, after you have spoken with him, any questions I will be free to answer and answer honestly."

Right then, Diego, calls his dad back, and says, "Dad we need to talk? But I think in person. Momma only said, ask your dad; it was his decision."

Marvin says to Don Diego, "I can't hide forever and yes, son, we can talk. Can I check my schedule and get back with you and your sister? I am only going to tell this one time."

All that afternoon and going into the evening, I notice that Don Diego, just watches the phone; he watches the mainline; he watches his cell phone at one point even ask Darcell if their dad has called or texted her any information.

Darcell is puzzled but answers, "No," then says, "should he have?"

Don Diego says, "Forget it, he will call me."

Later into the night, Marvin does call him. They both realize spring break is approaching, and the twins will already be with him. Let's sat aside one of those days said Marvin. Don Diego did agree.

Two days later, I decide to tell Fredrick what has finally taken place, and to my surprise, two days ago, he too called his ex-wife to say that he was sorry. He told her that she is beautiful and always will be in his eyes. He then asks her for forgiveness. Beverly, who the Son has set free, is free indeed.

"Fredrick, we are on the same page," I say, "I love you. I just love me some you."

"Come over here, silly lady, and just give me a kiss."

He tells me that his ex-wife said she was more then a body; she was his wife, his lover, but most of all, she should have been his friend. She told him, "You were the one who wanted children right away. I went against myself knowing it was to soon, we were newlyweds. We got pregnant, then pregnant again." Kayla told him, "Now the only God I worship is God the creator, my Lord and Savior. I have forgiven you, moved on, I thank you for this time and will accept your apology. Fredrick, it was only four years into the marriage and my weight was the issue, sorry I couldn't lose it, if you should see me now still pump and sexy. Your cheating disrespected me, you crushed me inside and out, you made me ashamed to be me, but God said that he was the only God I should have idolized. Fred, it is okay, time has healed this wound."

Fredrick's Truth

Our past marriages revealed

Although Fredrick said we would talk openly and honestly, well, we never did; we spent our time in fun and enjoyment. There is a time for everything, as the Bible states our time has come.

It has been almost a year and what a year for me. Fredrick loves to have fun; we go to plays and concerts, movies and dinner plays, more comedy shows back and forth, to New York for Broadway plays. My time with him is always full of gratification.

This day it is raining outside, and Fredrick called me over to his place and so I go, knowing that something is troubling him. I knock on the door. He opens it and greets me with a kiss and a hug. Although still loving, I feel somewhat uncomfortable.

"Good-looking," I say, "what is going on? You just don't seem like yourself."

"Beverly for the last past two days I have been talking to my mother telling and expressing my love for you. She then asked the question, 'Son, you must put it all out there, have you been honest, have you been faithful?'" He gives me a crooked smile. "I told her yes, she then said, 'Do you really love her the way she is?' I pondered, but I said yes, I do.

"Beverly, I called you over to talk about me, about my life before you and about me now. I know we talked about our ex-spouses apologizing and me apologizing to mine, but today is different. This is upon my heart as a man, and as a man who might want to reach further into this relationship. First, I was married for five years, had two beautiful little girls; my wife was such a beautiful woman. After the girls were born, she never really looked the same in my eyes. I wanted what I wanted, and that was for her to look the same, nothing less."

"Fred, what are you saying!"

"Please, Beverly, just listen. My wife gained so much weight after the children; I no longer found her attractive. So I started to cheat and cheat, destroying my marriage, wiping away my love for her. She even suggested going to counseling, and I remember saying, 'What size would you be then, big girl?' then just slamming the door and leaving. My lady on the side Maria looked the part. Maria is what I thought I wanted on my arms; she had no children, a good job, and made me happy in every area of my life. After I packed up and left my wife, Maria and I had a ball, until six months later. I told her how much I loved her, and she told me that she was fond of me. Fred, you left the mother of children because she gained weight. 'That could have been me!' she screamed. 'No, this is not real, it was fun while it lasted, Fredrick. I really don't want a forever life with you. Man, your life has been full of cheating and thinking that it was okay, sorry, Fred, that was doggish behavior; you are not the one for me.'

"Beverly, I am no longer that man, I realized it the day of the accident. I saw you, a beautiful you. This year has been the best year for me in a long, long time."

"Fredrick, you were that stuck on size?" I say, but he never answers.

"As my business developed and I thought that going to big corporate parties, I wanted a certain kind of woman on my arms who could wear any type of dress and look marvelous. Silly me, oh, silly me." As I go to hug and comfort him, he pulls me so tight and says, "I love you, I love you." He kisses me so hard. "Please never leave, you are the one who will be on my arms and have been in my arms." Tears roll down his face at that time.

I say, "Baby, now you listen to me. I was married and had the world, so I thought. Doctors after doctors told me as a teenager I will not be having any children, so when I met my husband he told me that he never wanted any children, just a wife to spoil, a wife to come home to, a wife to make love over and over, a wife to travel and a wife to be his best friend. I said I hit the jackpot and for years that is how it was, wonderful. Fredrick, one day while in London, I thought I would tell him the best news in the world, a miracle, I thought. I have never been able to tell a soul about this, Fredrick, you must be special to me." Tears start to form in my eyes and voice shaky, I continue. "To my surprise, he told me to get my ass on the next plane regardless of the cost, and when he returned home the pregnancy should be no longer. He told me that I was a liar and I only wanted to trap him because he was such a good catch. The more I tried to explain, the more my voice became like an echo in his ear. He hated me; it took him 15 years to apologize. I have been in and out of therapy for years; you are the only man I have ever really allowed myself to go out with and truly I have enjoyed this year. So, hearing your truth and you hearing my truth, what does this do for us? Two scared people afraid to love again, two scared people were wandering around, hoping to love again. You see, Fredrick, those lives were in the past, and for me I am tired of looking back, how about you?"

At that time, we both look at one another and at the same time say, "I love you."

"Bev, if you ever had a baby, you can believe afterward I am still going to love you."

"Fred, I know your issue with weight is over because I am that chunky, sexy creation who you now love."

During the year we have touched a little, kissed a little, but tonight it feels different, we both are free.

Fredrick looks into my eyes and says, "Beverly, can tonight be a different night? I want you," and I say slowly, "I want you too."

This night we both give in with emotions running wild. I tell him as he begins to undress me, "It has been years."

Fredrick says, "I know how to take care of you."

I allow Fredrick to explore all of me.

Spring Break

He is still my dad

The week of spring break, Marvin gets together with the twins, and they have a ball. On Thursday, Darcell comes back home. She says to me, "Momma, I don't want to hear about what went on plus Don Diego said that he would tell me, so I am home. They will be going out tomorrow talking man to man."

I ask Darcell, "Are you sure? You too have the right to know and hear for yourself."

She still says no and mentions again that she will wait for her brother. "He will tell me all I need to know, not leaving out any details, but for now, I am tired. My day has been long, and exhausting I need to rest." Darcell says, and she proceeds to march up the stairs.

It is Friday morning, and Don Diego gets up, takes his shower, and he prays, knowing that today will be a day of truth. *What will I think when this is over? Who ended the marriage? Was it, momma or dad?* He thought to himself. Everything enters his brain. He even wonders why Darcell doesn't find this necessary to stay and listen. *I'm not mad at her; maybe just too much for her to hear and bear. She loves both momma and dad,* he answers for Darcell.

"Good morning, Don Diego, what would you have me cook for breakfast? Our day is busy and long, important, and yet complicated," says Marvin.

Daydreaming, Don Diego can hear his dad, but he can't respond quickly. "Yes, Dad, what were you saying? Sorry."

Marvin says, "No problem, what would you like for breakfast?" Marvin tells Don Diego, "I would be lying if I said I was not afraid, I don't want to lose my children, and this can cause a rift between the three of us."

Don Diego says, "I will take bacon and eggs over easy and pop in a waffle or two. Dad, don't look at this as the end but say it is the beginning."

"Are you the father and I am the son? Thank you, son, I feel so much better," Marvin responds.

Finally, it is time to leave, and Dad says, "Should I talk while I drive, or should we sit down and have lunch? Which do you prefer, Don?"

"On our way, if it is okay, Dad, I will start the conversation. Momma was very upset, and I could see it on her face as she handed me the home line. I only caught the last part of the conversation she was having with you. She said that you loved us but stopped loving her. Is that the reason you never called the house or had any interactions with her, talking only through Grandma and my three aunts for all these years? I have never asked Mom; however, I always thought it to be strange, just never inquired. However, now I am, Dad. I need you to tell me."

"Don, are you sure you want to hear this from me?"

"I think my mother has suffered in silence," says Don Diego.

"And who says that I have not?" Marvin responds somewhat angrily.

"Dad, we are here to talk not hurt but talk."

At that time his father pulls over and calls the house. Beverly, do I have your permission to speak openly and honestly to him? She says yes, although she had given him the go-ahead already.

Don Diego listens as his dad speaks to him like never before.

"Dee, I was wrong, but I really couldn't control myself," his dad starts out. "When I left the marriage I was hurt, I was angry, I was so confused, and I was out of control. My anger turned into pure bitterness.

"Right after I left, I was offered a great assignment to go to Paris for six months to prepare an old theater, the Ateliers Berthier, and get the place ready for the mass production. During that time, I meet Marcello, we went out, he took me places and around people I thought that I could never be around, frankly could hardly stand to look at them and now I was invading their space. Fortunately, I got to see people for who they are, not sissies or fags, not real boys, as I called lesbians, but men and women who have chosen to live, not judge but live."

Stunned, Don Diego quickly interrupts, "Dad, are you gay?"

"No, son, I am not, but I thought I was because of the way I reacted when your mother told me she was expecting. When I met Marcello, my whole life changed. He told me that he was in the life, meaning he was gay. Marcello had married a woman, they had no children. He told me that he could never please her no kind of way except when they were out and dressed up because of his good looks. Marcello was very handsome and knew it. One day he said, 'Finally I had to stop the charades, told my ex-wife the truth and I left.' The longer we went out, it was Marcello who said, 'Marvin, you need to stop playing charades, you are not gay. We have been together, and I have watched you, you never dance in the clubs with me or any other man; when I go to hold your hand, you pull it back; at times when I wanted to kiss you, you turned your head and walked away. My friend,' he said, 'you are running from something, your sexuality is not the reason.' 'Let's talk about your life.' I told him everything, he then suggested that I see a therapist. At first, I refused, until Marcello said, 'Marvin, you are the typical black man, scared to explore your most vulnerable inner self, let me say this and you hear me, man, to fly you must first be free.' After that we hung out in both clubs, gay and straight, we were just friends.

"When I came back home, I took his advice and called a therapist. In those sessions, I had to come to grips with the fact my father was absent and didn't want to play a role in my life. Don, I was badly affected by the absence of my father. So, when your mother said she was pregnant, fear gripped me, but anger took hold and my mind started running. I became like a volcano with hot lava erupting. How would I be as a father? Would I be like him? Why would you put me in such a predicament? Don, I can only say sorry and hope that is enough. It took me sixteen years to finally be free." (Tears fills Marvin eyes)

(Seeing the pain in his dad's eyes) Don Diego asks "Dad whatever happened to Marcello"

"Well, he got married, and he still lives in Paris. Whenever I am there, we go for lunch. He is my friend and will always be; he taught me what no other man have ever taken the time to teach me, be honest, be happy, most of all be free. Dee, it was never about your mother and my children; it was about a boy who never knew the joy of a father, a boy who was never taught to be a man. Your mother always mentioned the word miracle. I know now that is what you and your sister are, a miracle. Two miracles that I love and cherish, two miracles that I will do anything for, two miracles that brings me joy and a life of fulfillment. I thank God for my miracles. That is all your mother tried to express and explain, but I felt betrayed. I didn't want any children, I just wanted a wife to love and cherish. What hell I have lived in for all these years, destroying such a beautiful family that God blessed me with, I ended the marriage, not your mother."

Don Diego hugs his dad so tight, and they both cry tears of joy for one and tears of relief for the other.

"Who the Son has set is free is free indeed" (John 8:36).

The next morning, Marvin drops Don Diego off at home. When Don Diego enters the house, I am standing right there.

"Are you okay? How was your time with your dad?"

"Honestly it was honest, and you know, Momma, I don't need your side, he never lied, he never said a word against you, he only spoke about himself. Momma, my dad was confused and suffering at that time. Momma, oh momma he is still my dad. Sorry, your marriage didn't stay together. I love you, Momma. I love you," Don Diego says.

After inhaling all that, Don Diego needs to rest before he talks to his sister.

Several hours later, knock, knock, it is Darcell.

"Tell me what happened, what did Dad have to say?"

Don Diego sits up slowly, rubbing his face, and says, "Are you ready?"

"Yes, I am."

He begins to tell Darcell what a wonderful time he had with his dad, that is first, then he says, "Darcell, Dad only wanted Momma, no children. Momma had female complications and was told that she could not have children. Dad said he thought Momma lied after he told her that he didn't want any children. He just could not forgive her, and so the marriage ended. That is why all communications came through Grandma and our aunts. So, when he called her last month, it was the first time in years he had even spoken with Momma, but he called to apologize."

Darcell says, "Wow, after all these years."

"Sister, I said the same thing. Darcell, how are you feeling right now about the circumstances and the facts as they relate to us, because it was about you and me?"

At that moment she gives no answer, only mumbles, "Wow, he didn't want any children and got twins."

Don Diego becomes defensive and wants Darcell to know that their dad loves them and has always taken care and provided for them.

"We have traveled the world. Darcell, mistakes are made to be forgiven, he asked that of Momma, and in a way, he asked that of us."

Darcell says, "Don, can you forgive him?"

Don Diego says, "Yes, he is still my dad."

Darcell says, "Yes, I can, and like you said we all make mistakes, he is still my dad, too. I am going downstairs with my mother, are you coming?"

"Yes," says Don Diego, "but let me wash my face, I will be down."

"Momma!" yells Darcell.

"Yes?" I say.

"Are you okay, Momma? I don't know if you will forgive my dad, but he is my dad and I love him just as I love you. Will you forgive him, Momma, will you?"

"Darcell, it has been so long. It is now time for me to heal, so yes, forgiveness is in order. Where is my handsome son?"

"Here, right here, Momma," Don Diego says as he is walking down the stairs. "Momma, you are amazing, just an amazing woman of God." He runs over and kisses me on the cheek.

That night I thank God for my miracles. I also decide that night to tell the twins how I am beginning to feel about Fredrick. I know now I can talk to them and not be afraid that they will be mad or even jealous. Today has allowed me to see them as maturing young people, so proud of them.

My Woman

Fredrick has been cooking all day, a little of this and a little of that. He is nervous about what he is about to do. *I have examined me, and I now like what I see. Beverly is the woman for me, she makes me feel so alive, she gives me the life I thought that was gone forever. Father, God, you have had mercy on me, and I thank you. Everyone who I love my children, my ex-wife has forgiven me, and most of all I have forgiven me. So, Fredrick now is the time*, he says to himself.

He calls Beverly. "Hello, my everything, I was thinking of you. If you are not busy after work, can you make your way over to my house this evening?"

Beverly says, "Yes, by the way I am not at work today, nor am I teleworking from home. So, coming over later sounds good. Umm, let the twins get in from school and practice. I will be over shortly, is everything alright? I can come now.

"No, sounds great. I will see you when you get here, love you," says Fredrick.

I finally arrive; the twins had so much to say another school year. I ring the doorbell and I can hear him yelling, coming. Fred, you look and smell good what are you cooking up in here, I am ready to eat you and the food.

We both laugh, and I proceeded to walk towards the kitchen, he stops me and says tonight we will be dining in the formal dinner room. He brings out a platter of shrimps, he brings out salmon and mixed vegetables, he brings out noodles and a little rice.

As we dine over soft music and candlelight, I think about how this was once the norm when I was married. Tears slowly drop down my cheeks.

Fredrick says, "Why are you crying?"

"I feel love, these tears are tears of joy."

Fredrick softly kisses my lips and pulls me close to him and says softly, "My body wants you and my heart wants you, too." He then says, "Beverly, when change comes, foolishness is then put aside. I love you just as you are; if we are respectful, honest, and honor one another, our love will continue to grow just as flowers. Beverly," Fred says, "I lost in this life my first love, now after years I can see her real beauty. My ignorance put me in a life of whoring around and no real fulfillment, but you, I saw you as you, I love you, I really love you. Beverly Chase, would you be my wife?"

I don't answer right away because I am waiting for Fred to pull out the engagement ring. So, without the ring, I answer yes. He lifts me up so high, and then he gently kisses my lips, then Fred says, "No ring, tonight there will be a ring."

I say, "Baby, I was so afraid, afraid to live, afraid to love, being called a liar and other names by my ex-husband mentally he butchered me so bad that there was never a bandage big enough to cover the scar, but tonight I rip off the bandage. I love you, I love you, and yes, I will marry you, I will marry you."

In silence, we both cry. Our past lives kept us caged; our new life will set us free. We stayed stagnated because of our past. We both struggled to erase our old selves and start fresh. Now, Fred, we are happy; we are free from ourselves and others.

"The battle was finally won, Fredrick, it was won today," I say.

Instantly, I grab Fred's hand, sit down, and I start to talk about who we should tell first, or should we have a dinner party and announce the celebration?

"Fred, how do you want us to tell everyone, shout it on the mountaintop?"

"I don't care, Miss Hollywood, soon-to-be Mrs. Chase, however you want to you have my blessing. One thing I ask, can we not have a long drawn-out engagement? I want you and all of you."

I thank him for respecting my values for the last two years. Although at times I gave into temptation and maybe would have been judged by many, I continue to pray and ask God for strength in that area where I was so weak. Fred and I think it will be best just to end the evening with a kiss and him walking me to the door and putting me safely into my car.

"Mr. Chase?" I say.

"Yes?" he answers.

"We have met each other's children, but our children have not met one another." Let's plan a day when we all can get together as one family. What do you think, sweetie?"

Fred says, "I agree. Bev, can you start working on a plan with activities and I will send you a text what my girls like, and we have to go somewhere your son will have fun as well, he is the only teenage guy."

"Right," I say. "I will do that as soon as you send me the text. Give me a kiss, I am leaving."

We kiss goodnight.

I say, "I will call you when I get in the house."

Later during that week, Frederick calls me and tells me not to worry about finding a place. He said I would cook, and all of us will meet then; we need to save our money for our wedding. We both laugh, Fred, I agree. Can we also invite our mothers?

"Yes, Bev, "Now that sounds great. "

Fred, did you tell your girls that you had proposed?"

"Yes, I did, and Bev, did you tell the twins that I proposed to you?"

"Yes," I say, blushing, "yes, I did and they were happy for us."

"My girls were, too. 'Dad,' they said, 'Mom got remarried, why not you?'"

"Fred," I say, "we have awesome children."

"Yes, we do, talk to you later. I am somewhat busy," Fred says as he hangs up the phone.

I say, "Wait."

Fred answers, "I am preparing and working on this conference that is less than a month and a half away. Shirley is briefing me on all finalizations. We are making sure that the final approval from every vendor, and keynote speaker is signed and submitted on time."

"Sorry, babe, go ahead, love you," I say.

I Thought the Storm Was Over

"Momma, come over here now, I thought I could finally be happy, I thought I heard the church bell ring, I thought I could trust him. Momma, please answer," I say frantically, I say while staring at the phone. "Where are you, Momma?"

Maybe about two hours later, my mother does reply but in a stern voice. "Beverly, you need to calm down so that I may understand what you are crying and screaming over."

Still emotional, I slowly get myself together and am able to speak clearly to tell my mother what has happened. I start out telling my mother why I was calling Fred from the start.

"I was planning for the children to meet and wanted our mothers to come along as well, I was calling Fredrick to ask if he had any suggestions."

Momma says, no, you were not just calling me regarding planning a dinner. Crying and screaming, girl, skip over all the unnecessary details and tell me what is going on?

At this time, she is speaking to me in a tone that she hardly ever uses with me. I wanted to say Karen and not Momma.

Karen says to me, "Beverly, it is late, I need you to take a shower, and we can talk tomorrow, and by the way, where are the twins?"

Somewhat embarrassed, I say softly, "They are asleep."

Quickly she responds, "Do you want to wake them and cause them to be disturbed and began to see Fredrick in another way? Beverly, you better think, and goodnight."

Shocked, I am left holding the receiver, nothing but dial tone. My mother has hung up on me. I too hang up the phone and do as she had instructed, take a long, hot shower and say a prayer and I fall asleep.

Meanwhile, Fredrick is distraught, confused, and angry. He just doesn't understand why Maria, after almost two years, would appear at his door without any notice or purpose. Out loud he screams, "My life is so wonderful, why this and why now?" As he looks out of his window, he watches as the cops get back into their cars. Thirty minutes earlier he thought that he was on his way to jail. All he does know is an attorney is needed.

That night Fredrick tosses and turns, he finally just gets out of bed and goes into his seating room. His head is spinning. *Did I make a mistake?* he questions himself. Fredrick begins to go over the event in his mind. *I saw Maria in the grocery store two to three weeks ago. She said, "Hello, Fredrick, I haven't seen you in a while, how have you been?" I replied, "Just fine." Then out of the blue, she asked can she come over to my place, I know I said no because I am in a serious relationship. I remember she looked at me, then walked away and made some remark, I just shoved it off and continued shopping. Just out no where she decided to come to my home with an orange sheer duster and orange and cream high heels, talking about I miss you and one body part misses you the most, why didn't I just close the door? For one second, I became my old self, the lustful me. Maria said, "I am still that tiger, right now I am ready to pounce, so get on over here and take me to the juggle." "Maria, as I told you in the store, I am in a relationship, will you please leave?" calmly I asked her repeatedly. I guess because I didn't allow her to be a tiger in the loving sense, she became aggressive and attacked me. She scratched my face, ripped off my t-shirt, and then she started screaming, "You are going to screw me!!!" "Maria, I am a different man, in love with a different kind of woman, please just leave or I will be calling the police." At that point I felt violated and abused and anger was kicking in, and I wanted to hurt this woman, but instead I called the police.* Fredrick started to pace back and forth as he went over every detail in his mind. *Then if this nightmare isn't enough, Beverly is calling while I am opening the door for the police.*

Fredrick look at his phone, he starts not to answer but needs to hear her voice.

"Beverly, I am in a situation, the police are at my door, let me call you right back."

Beverly then says, "Do you need me to come over?"

"No," he says, "my old girlfriend showed up here and has attacked me violently."

"Why would she do that?" Beverly asks.

"Babe, I got to go now," he replies.

While hanging up, he can hear Bev asking, "Why was she at your house, Fred?"

"Officer, please come in, look at me, I am scratched up, this woman came to my house uninvited with this outfit on, yes, I let her in, then told her that I was in a serious relationship and that is when she attacked me."

"Excuse me," one of the officer's ask, "Do you know this woman?"

Again, Frederick answers, "Yes, we dated for a few years but I haven't seen or heard from her in a year and a half; about three weeks ago, I saw her in the grocery store. Can you remove her from my home? She refuses to go."

Then the officer says, "Miss, we will be taking you downtown and booking you. You have assaulted this man."

"Yes," says Maria, "I did without any regrets."

One of the officers at that time advises Fredrick to take out a stay-away order.

> *Fred, you got to think maybe Beverly was right. I should have never let that woman in, but the Federal Express truck was pulling into the driveway. Maybe I should have closed the door on him as well,* Fred says to himself. *Stop driving yourself crazy, you did as you did, just let this situation pass.*

Beverly

Two days have passed before Momma calls me back, then she says in a very concerned-like tone, "Beverly, you are getting too old to handle everything with so much emotions," screaming, yelling, crying, "Too much, Beverly, too much, what had Fredrick done? Did you speak to the man?"

For a second, I say nothing, then I say, "Momma, no, I have not, when he told me that the woman was in his house, and that the police were there I just lost it, why would some woman be at your house; Momma, he had to have let her in?"

"So, what, do you know the circumstances, or did you just assume the worst?"

Again, Momma's questioning silences me, and I can only answer, "Maybe I jumped to conclusions and from there I went crazy. But Momma, I did not cuss Fredrick. I only asked the question, why you let that woman in your home? I hung up before he could give a response. I have not spoken to him since that evening, and he has not reached out to me either. I thought he loved me!"

Momma says, "Beverly, you needed a sister or a brother. I am the only child and you are an only child."

At this time, Momma keeps on talking. I do have my cousins, who are like my sisters, especially Damita. We go out; we talk about serious issues; we laugh about all things.

"Beverly, who do you confide in other than me, your mother?"

"Momma," I say, "Patricia I can talk to and I love being with Ness, but Momma, I miss 'real talk,' that was my time. I have been so angry at the person who leaked and told Patricia's husband what was said. Momma, do you think that person wanted him? What reason or motive made her say anything?"

"Baby, some women are outright stank and whorish and would do all they could to break up a good marriage when they think someone has a good man."

"Momma," I say, "you did not have to go that low."

Momma, says, "Beverly, you mean to tell me; you still don't know who told?"

"Momma, that is the truth," I respond.

"Scandalous, I mean scandalous!" she shouts.

The both of us just laugh.

"Momma, you are everything to me, thank you. I am going to get my thoughts together and call Fredrick,"

"Okay, Bev, don't lose a good thang using old tactics. Talking is the key. I got to go." Momma says all that as she is hanging up and on her way to exercise class.

"I sure do love that lady," I quietly say to myself.

Scars on the outside, scars in the inside

Fredrick looks at his face, his hands, and his chest, still in disbelief. *I am all scarred from a woman that I haven't seen in years. Scarred by someone who I was willing and did allow to get between my marriage. I now understand the old wives' tale "The grass is not always greener on the other side." Maria, Maria, you have lost your mind.*

As Fredrick continues to rub the cocoa butter over his body and his face, still talking aloud, "How long before these scars will disappear? I have a conference in two weeks, and I am one of the keynote speakers. Let me get out of my own head and fix me some breakfast."

At that time the doorbell rings, ding, dong.

"Who is it?" he yells and eases to look out of the peephole, it is Bob.

"What in the hell, man, you are mess up and marked up, did you get any licks?" Bob jokes.

Fredrick tells Bob, "Man, this shit is serious, and you come over here joking, why didn't you call first?"

"I thought you liked pop-ups," Bob says, this time laughing at his own self. Then Bob says, "No, man, I am just being silly. I know this is serious. Fred, what happened?"

Still somewhat irritated, Fredrick starts to speak. "I saw her about two to three weeks in the store; we said hello, that was all, no long, drawn-out conversation, just hello. Then the other day, out of the blue, I got in from a meeting, walked into the kitchen, looked in the refrigerator, then the doorbell rang. I opened the main door but stood in the entryway. There she stood with a sheer orange duster on with nothing underneath. Bob, man, I was hesitant, but the Federal Express dude was pulling into the driveway."

Bob quickly interrupts Fred. "What was said?"

Fred says, "Nothing, I just told her to come in and have a seat. After the dude gave me the packages, I sat them down. I looked at Maria, then I asked, 'Why are you here?' Bob, I will not lie for a second, I wanted to rip off that orange duster, but I thought you are not the same. 'Again, Maria, why are you here? My life has changed so since the last I saw you. I am in love with someone and she is all I need, and she is all I want.' Man, this woman said, 'I came here for only one part of you and that part of you only.' She then jumped up and started pulling on my pants. At that point I did push her off me. I said politely, 'Would you please leave,' she attacked me like a tiger going after its prey."

Bob says, "Fred, did you hit that b***?" as he stands up. "Did you knock her out?"

"No," says Fredrick, "it was at that time I called the police. You could hear her in the background screaming, 'Call them, you are going to F me!!' 'Maria, please leave, I am bleeding all over the place, please leave now before you get hurt, I screamed! When the cops got here, that sheer orange thing was wide open. They asked her to close it and she said to them, 'No, he is going to F me!' One of the officers asked me if we could go to another room so that he could ask me some questions as the other officers dealt with Maria. He asked me did she live here, 'No,' I said, 'I haven't seen her in a year and a half, about two to three weeks I ran into her at the store.' Bob, just like I am telling you, we only said hello. Suddenly a woman officer came, and she appeared to be kind. I heard her ask Maria, can she please close her duster? What I could see Maria nodded yes, she was in a daze, saying nothing as the handcuffs went around her wrists. Bob, I am talking about a prideful, intelligent woman. Maria degraded herself, and her behavior mortified me."

Then Bob says, "Fred, what has Beverly said about all of this?"

"Well," says Fred, "she called in the midst of it all and could hear Maria screaming, so before I could say a word, she said, 'What is going on in your house?' All I could get out was 'Maria is here and I had to call the police. Beverly, let me call you back,' then she screamed, 'Who let her in the house?' And she hung up. Bob, I have not spoken with her in two weeks. I thought Bev loved me and could trust me, but her response was over the top, and to cut me off like that screaming, for what, let me call you back, was that too much to ask?"

Bob says, "Are you just giving up on Beverly because of that? Remember man the key is connecting, talk."

Fredrick slowly says, "No, I hope not. I know now that I love her, I am just trying to give her and myself a little space. Bob, I have done some awful things in the past, but this has left me so humiliated. I can't even imagine what made that woman come here. I did take out a stay-away order; I must go to court because the cops saw visible marks only on me."

Bob then says, "Fred, are you pressing charges?"

Fred explains to Bob that he is forced to because of the visible marks that the police witnessed. "Plus I think it is best."

Bob, at this time, was outdone. He apologizes to Fred for playing earlier. "Man, this is serious, do you know your whole life could have been turned upside down? Your business destroyed, your house, and your timeshare gone? This woman came to sabotage all you have worked for, man, I am so glad you handled that situation in that manner." Bob says, "I got to go but I will be keeping you in my prayers. What did Paul say in Romans 7:21, 'I find then a law, that, when I would do good, evil is present with me'? Fred, you keep me posted and stay strong, call Beverly, you two need to talk," Bob says before closing the door.

"Thank you, man," Fredrick says to Bob. "I haven't spoken to anyone except my mother."

Bob then turns around and chuckles. "Still a mommy's boy."

Fredrick chuckles as well but answers, "Damned right, holler at you later."

As he closes the door, Fredrick realizes at that time how he needed to talk to someone, and Bob was the right person at the right time.

Later that day, Fred thinks about what Bob had said: Connecting is the key, talk. "If I cannot talk to Beverly regarding this matter, how can we get married? Circumstances will occur, and together, not apart, we will need to address the situation. I will reach out to Beverly, we need to talk," he says aloud.

Frozen

As hot as it is outside, Fredrick receives a call from Beverly, ring! As he answers the phone, "Hello?"

"Fredrick, this is Beverly, and I think we need to talk to see where this relationship is going or not going. So, with your schedule, when are you free?"

Fredrick answers, "Currently I am not working and therefore my time is free until Monday, and you?" he also says in a harsh tone.

"I am not working today," Beverly says.

"Beverly, if you can come over to my house, that would be just fine."

"What, come to your house?" she says sarcastically.

"Look, Beverly, if there is a problem, then don't come. I just cannot at this time, do you want to talk or not?" angerly Fredrick replies.

"I am on my way now, Fredrick," she responds, realizing that Fredrick is in a different space and how things can easily go south.

I arrive after about 30 minutes. I sit in my car, comb my hair, then put on some lipstick. I had worn the lowest-cut top I own with the best pushup bra showing cleavage for days. I know that Fredrick loves my breasts.

As I am walking toward the door, Fredrick opens the door. He is looking out of the window and can see me getting out of my car. We greet one another as though we are strangers and meeting for the first time. We both exchange hellos, no kisses, no hugs, just hellos.

"Fred, it has been two weeks and I haven't heard anything from you," I start the conversation.

"Do you see my face, look at my chest and arms." He tears open his shirt and holds out his arms. "How can I meet with clients looking like a cat has attacked me? Beverly, I thought that you loved and trusted me; you hung up screaming why did I let a woman in my house? That lady came to my door unexpected with an orange sheer duster and no clothes underneath. At the same time Federal Express was delivering packages, what was I to do? That woman said that I was a dog and that she just played me for my money after leaving my ex-wife, thinking we had something strong."

I try to interrupt, but Fredrick says, "No, you sit and listen to me. Love means hearing someone out all the way, not just what you want to hear and then assume. The old me, Fredrick Marcus Chase, would have pulled her into this house and would have screwed her from one end of this house to the other. I can say that I love you so much I was able to tell Maria; look, I have someone who I now love. Beverly," Fred says, "all I asked you was to wait until the police had left, then I could have explained everything. One thing I do understand why my ex-wife couldn't trust me because I wasn't worth trusting. You, I have tried to show by my actions, and you still found me blamable."

"No, no, Fredrick," says Beverly, "I was wrong, I love you, Fredrick, and should have never doubted you or at least given you the chance to explain that situation, baby, please, I am sorry," and I run into his arms. We kiss and hug and for a while just holding one another.

Fredrick then fills me in on the upcoming court case, saying that he wouldn't have filed charges; however, the police were called and witnessed for themselves how crazy Maria was behaving. "She was arrested and charged with assaulting me and disorderly conduct toward an officer."

I keep touching his face. "The marks are healing, just continue to put on cocoa butter, and do you have any aloe vera gel?"

Fred says, "No, I have been using that medicated Vaseline."

"Okay," I say, "but you need the other two as well, I will get them for you. Nurse Bev is here. Baby, that scorned woman tried to scar my man's handsome face."

Fred smiles a little and replies, "Tried she did, Bev. I must leave for a conference in two weeks. I can't be on a business trip looking like I have been in a fight with a cat."

"I know." In my mind Fred needed me and I was not there, how can I make up for that? "Fredrick, I am staying the night, the twins are gone for another week."

Frederick tells me that he is in a vulnerable state and that staying would be challenging to him.

"Fred, thank you for being honest with me, but you need me, I will cook dinner for us, and we will watch TV, no more talking about that situation and any other situation for the rest of this evening," I insist.

After dinner and watching a little TV, I say, "Fred, do you have a t-shirt for me, I am getting sleepy."

Fred gives me a t-shirt. Normally I would go sleep in another room but tonight I tell Fred, "I am sleeping with you."

Fred never says a word on that, but he asks me if we can take a shower together, without any hesitation. I say yes, knowing that this will lead to a night of passion, in which we had decided together to hold off on sex until the wedding day.

Fred says, "Beverly, you know where this will be going."

"I know, Fred," I say.

"After tonight we can't, we must be strong and stick to what we have agreed."

"I strongly agree," I say, "but no woman comes to my man house and proposition him, no woman."

The shower is relaxing and inviting. We both take turns washing the other and in between kisses and exploring and exploding, Fourth of July has come again and what a bang. From the bathroom to the bedroom, it is that kind of night, a night to remember. Our love is tested and true love passes the test.

The engagement party

We do so much planning, and finally, the evening comes. We rent a small mansion that has several rooms. I wear a long fitted orange dress with plunging neckline and a split on one side. My hair has long extensions and makeup is slightly applied. I look beautiful and feel that way as well. Fredrick wears a designer shirt and some black fitted slacks, his haircut is a well-defined shape-up as though someone put a two-edged sword to his head, such an attractive man.

The place is packed; everyone came out. I notice that Patricia and her husband are there but no Monica. Patricia is honest and tells me that if Monica is coming, then she would have to decline.

"I read between the lines and decided that a code of trust was broken, and that Monica needed not be here or the wedding because her tongue was sharper than a two-edged sword."

Momma calls everyone to the orange room; it is time to play games. She asks, "Who wants to play ring hunt? If so, please go to the green room, and if you want to play bean bag toss, stay in this room." Giving out instructions is what Momma loves to do. "There is a time when we all must meet back in the main hall, where dancing and other fun activities will be taking place. Everyone has 45 minutes before meeting back in the main hall, thank you," Momma says, "let the fun begin. As for the couple, each one will be in a room, so go talk it over with each other."

Fred and I go over in the corner. I say, "I am with the ring hunt."

"Great," says Fred, "the bean bag toss I got."

Finally, the games are over, and we give out prizes to the winners. Time to go into the main hall. Fred and I have been ordered by our mothers not to see the main hall. We are the last to enter. Breathtaking décor, real flowers, the centerpieces, the chair covers, just beautiful.

As we walk in, overwhelmed I start crying. Fred kisses my forehead and says, "This is our life, beauty will follow us, my queen will forever cry happy tears. I promise you, baby."

Linda, who is Fredrick's mother, gives instructions as to where the drinks are, only wine and champagne, nothing heavy. Then she calls up Patricia and Ness. I don't know what they are about to do. Patricia takes the microphone, says a few words, then she and Ness belts out a Donna Summer song, "Last Dance." I scream, although I was not born when the song first came out I just love it. I clap and clap as the ladies sing that song.

I run to the front, give them a hug, then I take the microphone. "I am so happy, my husband-to-be is so glad, our children are tickled-pink, my mother and Fred's mother, they are so elated to see their children at peace and in love."

Fred's secretary is so funny, she walks up front, gets the microphone, and speaks on how much she loves him and how he has grown. Then different people begin to yell out, "I am happy for you, man, you deserve this, Beverly."

Lastly, before the evening has ended, my Fredrick, in front of everyone, kneels down on one knee. "My darling," he says, "thank you for accepting me, and my children, what a wonderful person you are, and what a blessed man I am." I can only cry as Fredrick asks his daughters to come over. Candy hands him a box and before he opens it he asks that Darcell come over, but he says to Don Diego, "I didn't buy your mother any type of engagement ring. I bought her one meant for a queen." Fred then shows Don Diego the ring. Then quickly, he turns back around, asks me for my hand. He slowly slips the ring onto my finger.

I start screaming, "It is gorgeous, it is gorgeous, what a ring."

The mothers run over to look. "Bling, bling, Beverly, you have hit the jackpot," Momma says loudly.

Fred's mother brags about her son. "What a man, I must say so myself, bling, bling."

Then some of the women and men get up to look and admire the beauty of the ring.

Ness whispers in my ear, "You see, little girl, some fairytales really do come true."

The rest of the evening is dancing and mingling. Fredrick and I thank every guest, then we look at one another, passion fills the air, but we decide to honor what we have agreed to, no more sexual contact until marriage. We kiss, Fred walks me to my car Don Diego is the driver, gives me another kiss, and says, "Goodnight, soon-to-be bride," and I say, "Goodnight, soon-to-be husband, no more separation, we will be together to live as one, to love as one, and to be one family."

The Wedding

I get out of bed, run to the mirror, "Today is the day that I become Mrs. Fredrick Chase, God, my Father, thank you, I give you glory and honor for giving me happiness."

I am so full that I thank God for putting into my spirit to have my hair done at my old salon, remembering my hairstylist. "She's gone but not forgotten. This morning I will be going into the salon where she worked. I wanted her to be a part of this celebration." My heart becomes heavy, and while I am wiping the tears away, Darcell comes into the room.

"Momma, are you ready? We got to go."

"Yes," I say, "I am ready to get this hair done, and be all dolled up for the man." "Then why did you look so sad when I walked into the room?" Darcell says.

"Not sad, baby, but thinking about Tonya and wishing that she was the one who would be glamorizing me for this occasion."

"Momma, you are right, she would have laid that hair today, I miss her too, Momma, she was so nice and funny, too."

We both laugh and say, "Okay, let's go get beautified."

"Today is the day that I take my new wife, Mrs. Fredrick Chase, God, thank you for forgiving me and allowing me a second chance at this thing called marriage."

Bob comes into the room. "Who are you talking to, Fred?"

"The Lord, Bob, the Lord," answers Fredrick.

"No issue here, man, who else can you take this to? Let's roll, get your hair cut, and pick up our monkey suits."

Fredrick pats Bob on the shoulder. "I love you, man, but there is only one you and you have a way with words."

The two giggles, and off they go to become appealing and, yes, dapper is the way to describe them the next time they would appear.

As I walk into the salon, the young lady greets me. “I am Tasha,” she says, “and you must be the bride, hello, Beverly.”

I say, “Hello.”

Instantly she makes me feel so welcome. For a few minutes, we talk about Tonya, and Tasha tells me that she didn’t get to know her very well, but the times they did talk, Tonya was always pleasant and willing to give her advice. I just say, “And for her clients, no hair was ever left out of place, not one strain, so I came here in honor of her.”

“What a touching testament to the person she was while she lived, I hope one day someone would pay homage to me,” replies Tasha.

The young lady does a fantastic updo with pieces of hair flowing down to the middle of my back, and Darcell’s hair is similar. We leave the salon looking doll-like, tip Tasha and tell her we will be back again. Tasha gives me a hug, “And best wishes to you today and forever.”

As the limousine pulls up to the church, Darcell, my mother, and I get out of the car; hurry to the empty room that had been prepared just for the bride. Beautiful flowers are there and the maid of honor, my cousin LaBelle. LaBelle is breathtaking; she has smooth chocolate skin. She is tall and slender looks as though she has appeared on the cover of every fashion magazine.

LaBelle’s voice is so light. “Beverly, let me check, bouquet, got it, rings, got them, garter belt, got it, gown elegant, now it is showtime.”

LaBelle gently helps me into my gown, and because she also is a makeup artist, she dresses my face as well. Then stands back and says, “Beverly, this is what God meant when he made women. You are stunning, and by your new husband’s side, you will be all he will ever need for the rest of your lives.”

I try not to shed a tear and shake my head to acknowledge LaBelle.

The people are arriving at the church, the groom and groomsmen are at the church, the ring bearer is at the church, but where is the bride-to-be?

Fred keeps asking everyone, "Has she arrived?" then his mother knocks on the door. "Your bride has arrived." It is another 15 minutes before the wedding ceremony.

As I stand in the doorway, I wait for the pianist to play "Here Comes the Bride." I close my eyes and think about my life and how I thought that I could never love again. A tear slowly falls down my cheek. Don Diego says, "Mom, are you ready?" "Yes, son, I am."

"Yes."

Slowly I take a few steps down the aisle, a version of loveliness, the beautiful goldish colored designer gown with a deep V showing cleavage, the bottom is a full ballgown. As I look up and there he is, the man who is about to become my husband. I stare at him but continue to walk down the aisle as Darcell recites this touching and an emotional poem that she wrote just for her mother.

"Here comes the bride in all her beauty, here comes the bride in all of her grace. There stands the groom, waiting to unite and become as one, may God join us together and bless this holy place. Here comes the bride in all her beauty, here comes the bride in all of her grace."

As we stand side by side, looking at one another, smiles so bright, the day outside is sunny and inside is sunny too because love is here with us. Then a voice like no other starts singing the Lord's Prayer, his tone is crystal clear like looking through glass, his name also is Don Diego, and he came highly recommended. His last song is "Flesh of my Flesh," chills run down my arms, and when I look over at Fredrick, big teardrops are falling down his face.

The guests applaud the singer as though he is giving a concert.

"Wonderful," says Bishop Jones. Bishop then cracks a few jokes before he gets into the meat of the ceremony. "These rings should never be taken off because the circle of marriage should never be broken, repeat after me."

As the Bishop reads us the vows, we say our "I do's."

"Then, you may salute your bride."

What a kiss he lays on me. Then we turn to our guests.

"Ladies and gentlemen, may I introduce Mr. and Mrs. Fredrick Chase," says the Bishop. As we turned to our guest, the applauds started congratulations, yes you did it, and I hear my mother say I praise God. As we walked down the aisle as Mr. and Mrs. Chase, we allow a few hugs and let the guests take some pictures before the professional photographers get started.

As the musician is leaving, I ask him to come and be in one of the pictures. Also, I ask if he will come to the reception and sing just one more song. Mr. Jones says, "If the reception is not too far from the church."

I answer, "Only ten minutes away, thank you so much; your voice is amazing."

Mr. Jones only smiles and takes a picture. Then, he proceeds to the church.

Mr. and Mrs. soon follow. The reception decorations fresh flowers, centerpieces, and balloons, magical. First, the small bridal party, then the couple of the hour, comes in with a bang. The dancing begins, we hug our children, other family members and friends, lastly, kissing our mothers on the cheek.

Fredrick and I both dance with our mothers for our first dance, then with our children, and lastly, with each other. We tell everyone to enjoy themselves, eat up as we leave for our two-week honeymoon in Hawaii.

We both say together, "I am the happiest man; no, I am the happiest woman."

Fredrick looks into my eyes and says, "What God has joined, let no man put asunder."

That night as we make love over and over, nothing but pleasure and passion, no more being uncomfortable about not living right, I say to my new husband, "Fred, you know, fairytales, sometimes they do come true."

Fredrick laughs and says, "My Cinderella, the shoe does fit, my Sleeping Beauty, you need to sleep no more, Frozen, my kisses of true love break the ice."

Then I say, "My Prince Charming didn't come on a white horse, he came through a fender bender."

We both laugh so hard.

"Okay," says Fredrick, "enough about fairytales, are we going to make a baby, or will you always be my baby?"

"I am your baby, and I pray this moment in time we lock love in our hearts. I love you, Mr. Chase."

"And I love you too, Mrs. Chase."

The lovemaking starts all over again.

The happy couple falls asleep. Fredrick wakes up, and not feeling his bride next to him, calls out her name. I come out of the bathroom with a sheer orange duster and high-heeled shoes.

Fred giggles and tells me, "You got jokes."

I say nothing as to why I changed into this outfit but know that Fred has gotten the joke. He pulls me over to him. We kiss, he slowly unties the belt, and seductively he lowers the orange duster and gently begins to lick me.

"Are you my lollipop?" he asks, and through all the moaning and groaning, I hardly can speak barely. I say, "Yes."

Early that morning we are leaving, we both take a shower together and as much as love is in the air, we know we have to get to the airport. I doze off in the limousine. Dreaming, Cinderella, he found the shoe, Sleeping Beauty, the kiss gives me life, Frozen love does overtake the heart.

I wake as we are pulling into the airport.

"Fredrick, is this a dream?"

"You tell me, I don't want to wake up, my baby, this is for real, and forever, I love you," says Fredrick as he gently kisses my forehead.

Epilogue

I wrote this book to inspire and to encourage people and women in particular. Know we are better than any storm that may come into our lives, any mountain of a situation we must climb. First, you must believe that Jesus will fix it; secondly, wait with patience, and hope an answer is coming. Thirdly, pray, "Lord, whatever the outcome keep me standing, I know that trouble doesn't last always."

Broken Beverly was thinking that she had married Prince Charming the first time around. You see, sometimes we see the dollar, and we see the success, but we forgot or just cared not to listen to the mess. It is the reason we should date to ask questions and be able to accept or reject the answers. Yet we find it better to focus on the looks, the sex, and the money. When you saw all the signs, yield, caution, slippery road, and stop, they were pointing, "don't go down that road." She experienced a miracle. Her ex-husband found it to be a nightmare. Beverly lived for the fairytale, not realizing some fairytales are not happy. So, for 16 years, she cried; at her lowest points, she ever wanted to die; however, she prayed for strength and raised her twins in love.

Oh, Fredrick, you should be ashamed, you had the best life, the best wife, and yet you couldn't accept the weight she gained after having the children. Success and love weren't enough; the trophy women, the right size, the right look, and yet the other woman, she crushed your manhood, not that you weren't handsome, successful, just that you were too doggish for her to make any commitment, so as the old saying goes, "the grass is never greener on the other side," Fredrick you forget to check.

Love, do we see it coming, well, they didn't, and it became a beautiful romance that ended in them starting the rest of their lives in marriage.

www.ingramcontent.com/pod-product-compliance
Lightning Source LLC
LaVergne TN
LVHW012023060125
800662LV00017B/611
* 9 7 8 1 6 4 7 0 2 5 3 8 0 *